PATTI FARMER ✳ JANET WILSON

What's He Doing Now?

FIREFLY BOOKS

To Bill and Trish — Trish for loving Lewis,
and Bill for being him.
— P.F.

In memory of my niece, Melanie Reid.
With special thanks to Navin
and the Malik family.
— J.W.

The illustrations in this book were drawn with watercolour pencil on Aquarelle paper.

This book was designed in Quark XPress,
with type set in 20 point Cushing Book.

A FIREFLY BOOK

Published in the U.S. in 1998 by:
Firefly Books (U.S.) Inc.
P.O. Box 1338
Ellicott Station
Buffalo, New York 14207

Cataloguing in Publication Data
Farmer, Patti
What's he doing now?

ISBN 1-55209-220-8 (bound) ISBN 1-55209-218-6 (pbk.)

I. Wilson, Janet, 1952-   . II. Title.

PS8561.A727W47 1998   jC813'.54   C97-932069-0
PZ7.F36Wh 1998

6 5 4 3 2 1   Printed and bound in Canada   8 9/9

In October, Lewis said to his mother, "We're going to have a what?"

1

"A baby," said his mother.

"A baby!" said Lewis. "Can I see it?"

"Not until May," said his father. "Your mother will deliver it in May."

"Like pizza?" said Lewis.

"Not exactly," said his father.

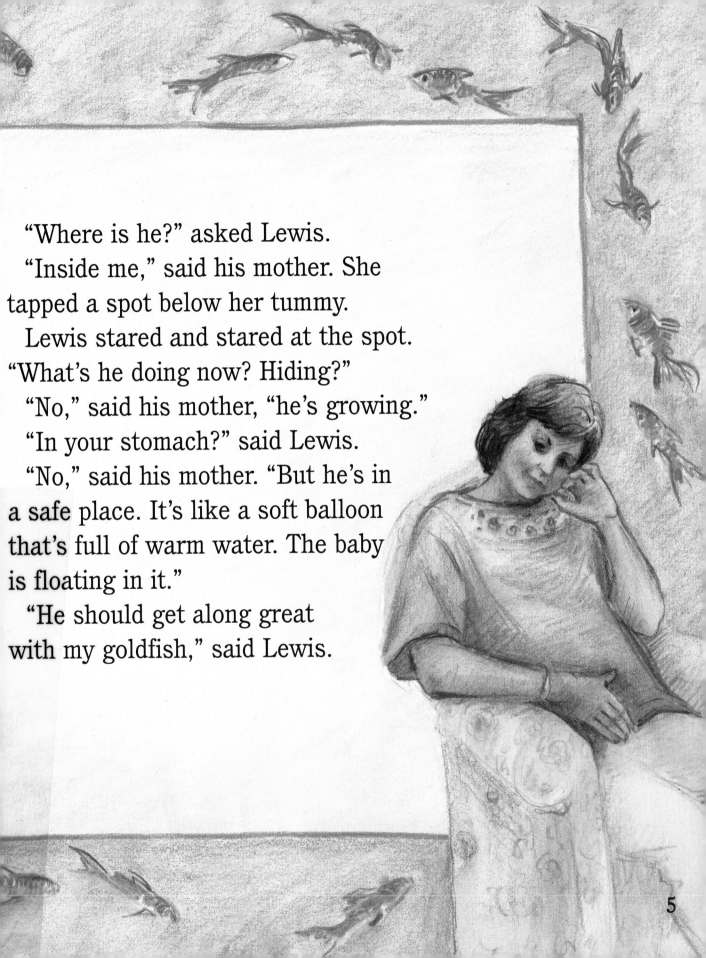

"Where is he?" asked Lewis.

"Inside me," said his mother. She tapped a spot below her tummy.

Lewis stared and stared at the spot. "What's he doing now? Hiding?"

"No," said his mother, "he's growing."

"In your stomach?" said Lewis.

"No," said his mother. "But he's in a safe place. It's like a soft balloon that's full of warm water. The baby is floating in it."

"He should get along great with my goldfish," said Lewis.

Later, Lewis was puzzled. "How can he breathe in there?"

"He doesn't need to breathe," said his father. "He won't breathe like you and me until after he's born."

"Oh," said Lewis. "Then he just kind of lies around in the water and grows."

"Yes," said his mother.

"He's going to look like a prune when he comes out," said Lewis.

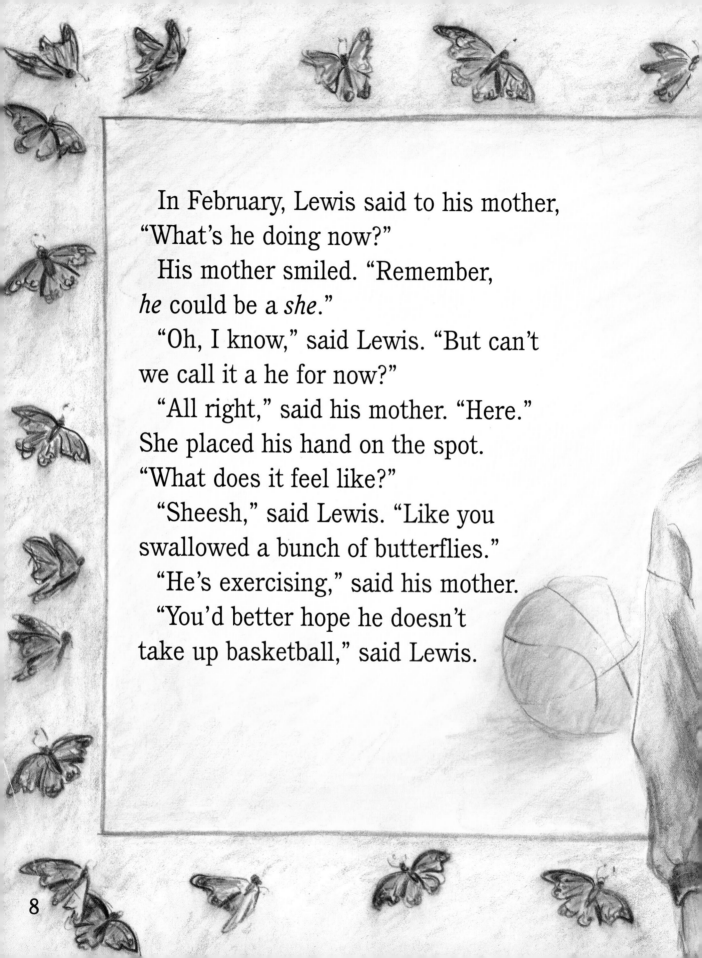

In February, Lewis said to his mother, "What's he doing now?"

His mother smiled. "Remember, *he* could be a *she*."

"Oh, I know," said Lewis. "But can't we call it a he for now?"

"All right," said his mother. "Here." She placed his hand on the spot. "What does it feel like?"

"Sheesh," said Lewis. "Like you swallowed a bunch of butterflies."

"He's exercising," said his mother.

"You'd better hope he doesn't take up basketball," said Lewis.

Later, Lewis went out for supper with his mother and father. "What does the baby eat?" he asked.

"He eats what your mother eats," said his father.

"Oh," said Lewis. "I'll have a hot dog."

"I'll have a hot dog, too," said his father.

"And I'll have the liver," said his mother.

Lewis looked at his mother. "Give the kid a break, Mom. Have a hot dog."

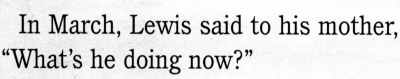

In March, Lewis said to his mother, "What's he doing now?"

"He's exercising harder," said his mother. "Feel."

Lewis put his hand on the spot.

"Yikes! I think he's fighting to get out."

"No," said his mother. "He's just growing bigger and stronger."

"Did I do that when I was inside you?" asked Lewis.

"Yes," said his mother.

"Sorry," said Lewis.

13

Later, Lewis helped his father put together the baby's crib and changing table.

"Dad," said Lewis, "do you think the baby will like me?"

"What baby wouldn't like a big brother like you?" said his father. "Think of all the things you can teach him, like walking, talking . . . "

" . . . and toilet training," said his mother. She plunked a large pile of diapers on the changing table.

"You mean, somebody has to teach him how to use the toilet?" asked Lewis.

"That's right," said his mother, smiling right at Lewis.

Lewis turned to his father. "Sounds like a good job for you, Dad."

In April, Lewis said to his mother,
"What's he doing now?"

"Well," said his mother, "He's just waiting
to get a little bigger and stronger before he's born."

"That's it?" said Lewis.

"No, wait," said his mother. "Listen."

Lewis put his ear to the spot. "What's that
thump, thump, thumping noise?"

"He's got the hiccups," said his mother.

"The hiccups?" said Lewis.
"I thought he was making
popcorn in there."

Later, Lewis helped his father put up the baby's wallpaper in the nursery.

"This seems like an awful lot of work," said Lewis.

"I know," said his father, "and you've been a big help. We just want everything to be special for the new baby."

18

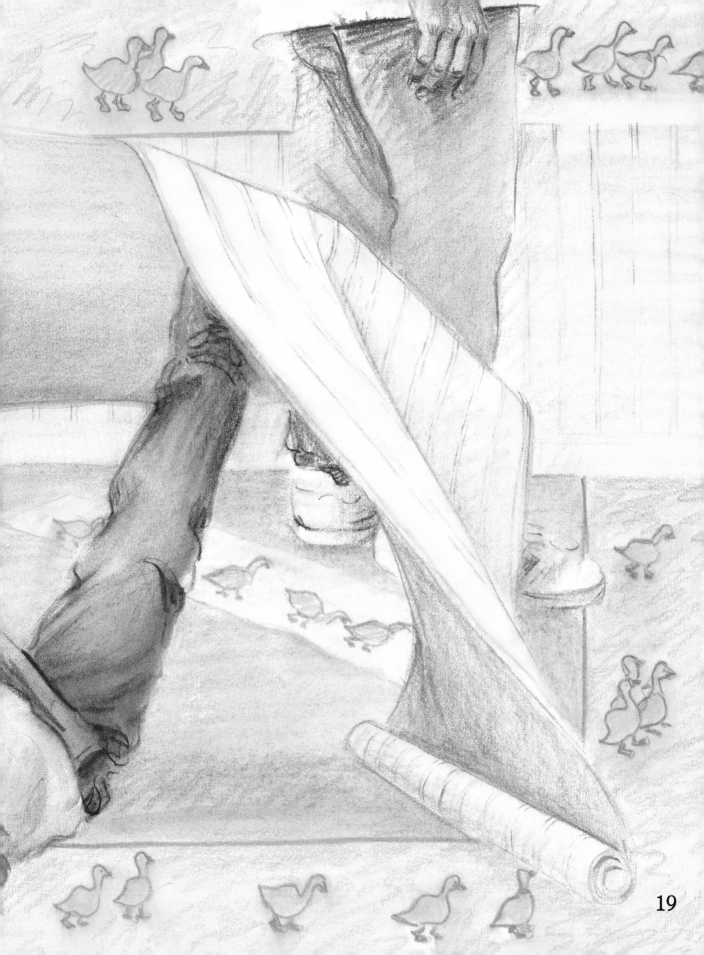

"Special, huh?" said Lewis. "Well, I guess I know where I stand in this family."

"That's right," said his father, kneeling beside him. "You're our number one son."

"And," said his mother, kissing him softly, "the first to be loved."

Lewis hugged them both.

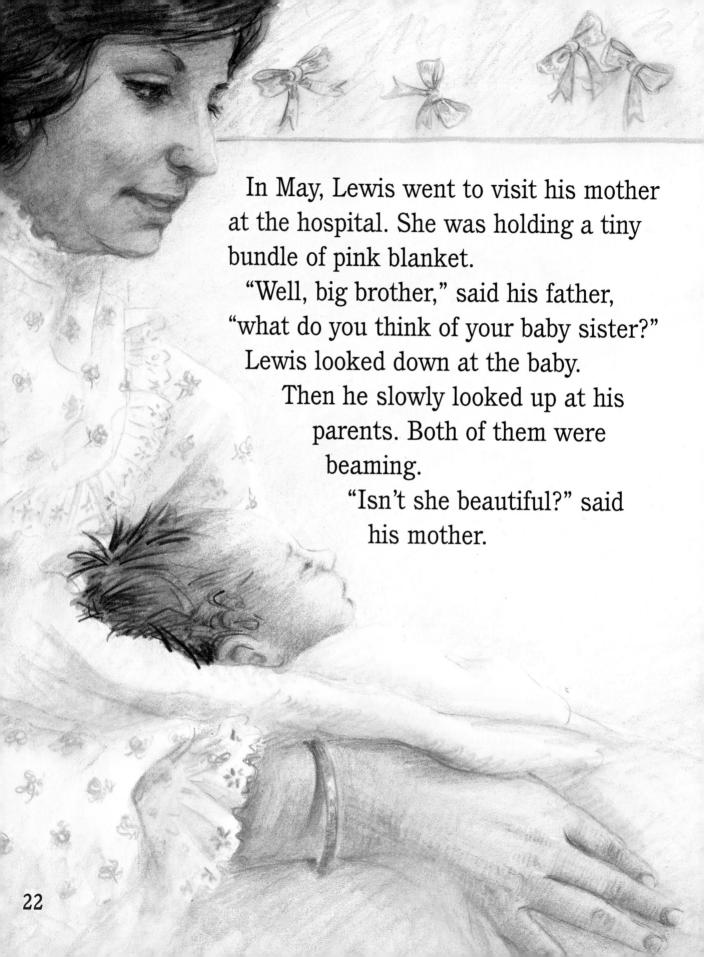

In May, Lewis went to visit his mother at the hospital. She was holding a tiny bundle of pink blanket.

"Well, big brother," said his father, "what do you think of your baby sister?"

Lewis looked down at the baby.

Then he slowly looked up at his parents. Both of them were beaming.

"Isn't she beautiful?" said his mother.

Lewis crossed his fingers
and said, "Yes, Mom, she's beautiful."

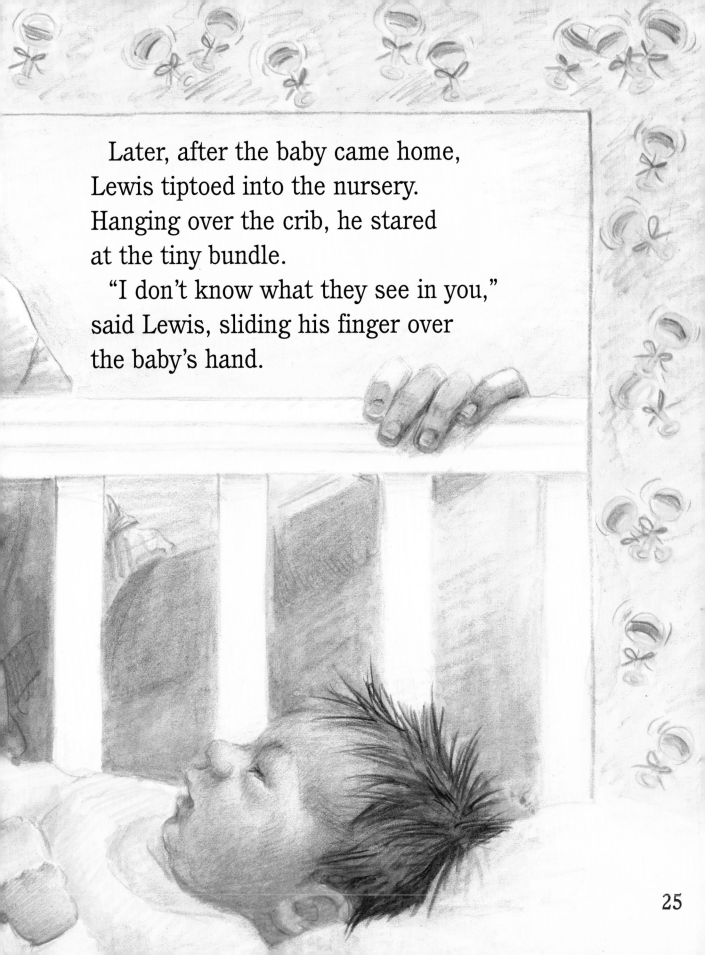

Later, after the baby came home,
Lewis tiptoed into the nursery.
Hanging over the crib, he stared
at the tiny bundle.

"I don't know what they see in you,"
said Lewis, sliding his finger over
the baby's hand.

Suddenly, she wrapped her tiny
hand around his finger and gurgled.
Lewis smiled and wiggled his finger.
  "But don't worry, Sis," he whispered.
"You won't stay a prune forever."

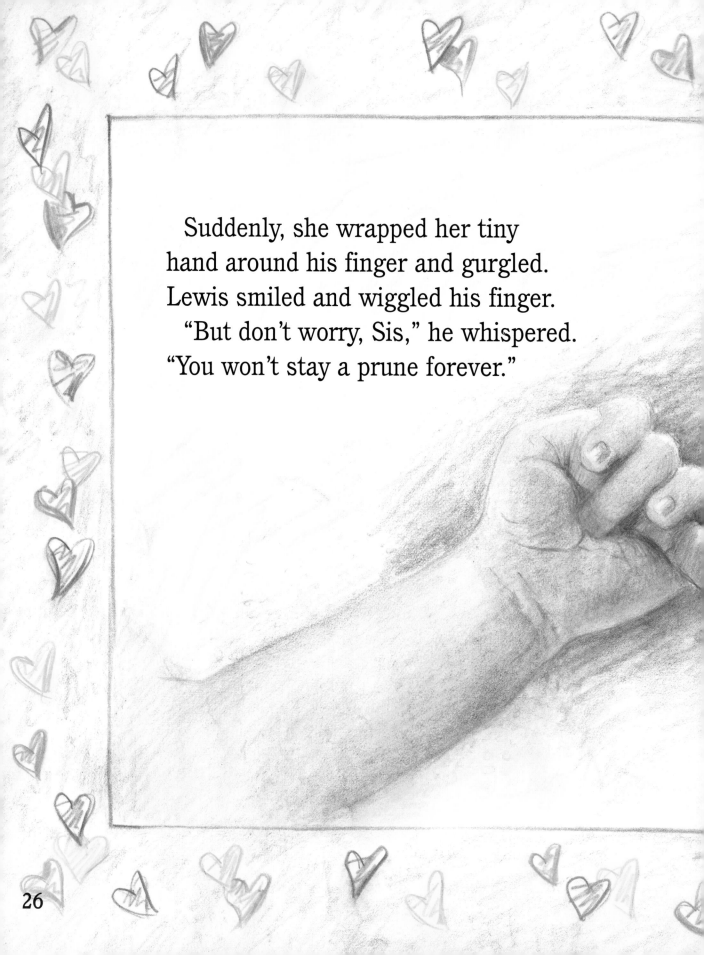

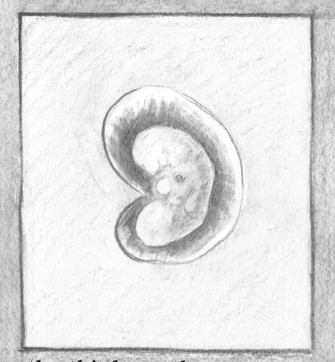

the third month

the fourth month

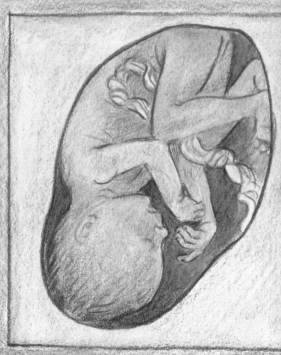

the seventh month

the eighth month

28

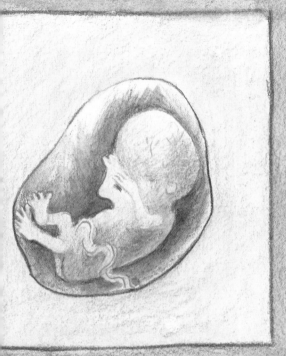

e fifth month   the sixth month

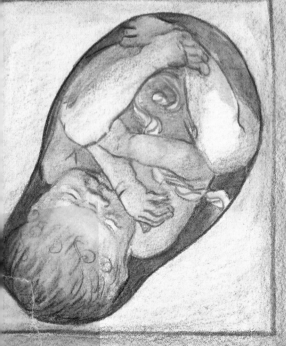

e ninth month   birth

29